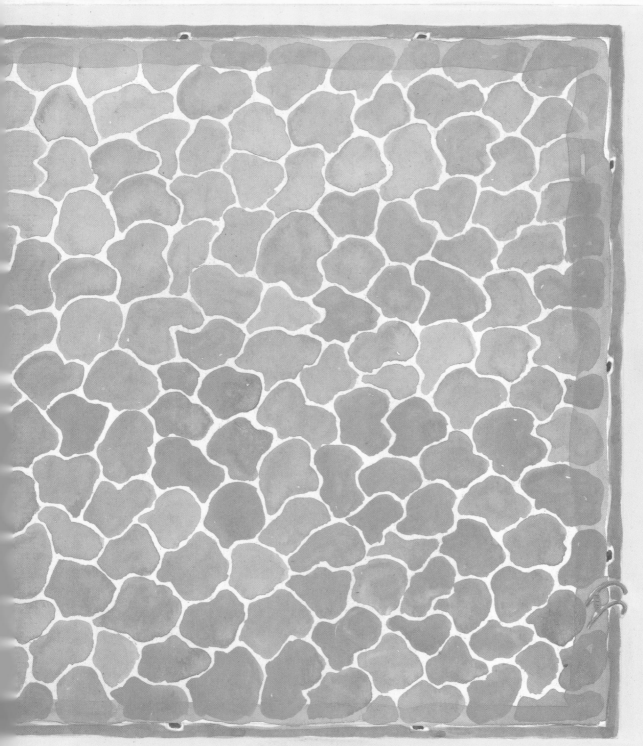

For my favorite synchronized swimmers,

Hannah, Elizabeth, and Julianna Joy
—A.R.

For Arnold and Nancy and swimming at the Outer Banks

—P.M.

Katie Catz Makes a Splash

Text copyright © 2003 by Anne Rockwell Illustrations copyright © 2003 by Paul Meisel
Manufactured in China. All rights reserved. www.harperchildrens.com
Library of Congress Cataloging-in-Publication Data
Rockwell, Anne F.
  Katie Catz makes a splash / Anne Rockwell ; illustrated by Paul Meisel.
    p.   cm.—(Good Sports)
  Summary: Fraidy Katie Catz learns to swim with help of Patsy Polarbear.
  ISBN 0-06-028441-2 — ISBN 0-06-028445-5 (lib. bdg.)
  [1. Swimming—Fiction. 2. Fear—Fiction. 3. Cats—Fiction. 4. Animals—Fiction.] I. Meisel, Paul,
ill. II. Title.
PZ7.R5943Kat 2003
[E]—dc21
                                                                          99-39893
                                                                          CIP
                                                                          AC
Typography by Matt Adamec
1 2 3 4 5 6 7 8 9 10
❖
First Edition

Katie Catz Makes a Splash

Anne Rockwell

illustrated by Paul Meisel

HARPERCOLLINS*PUBLISHERS*

"Hey! Katie Catz!" yelled Chip O'Hare.
"Come into the pool with us!"

"No thanks," said Katie.

"Nyah! Nyah! Fraidy Katie," said Chip,
and he dove beneath the water.

Everyone Katie knew was in the town pool,
but not Katie. Chip had said sharks and sea
monsters lived in the pool, and once, she'd
gotten water up her nose. Besides, Katie didn't
know how to swim. And that was fine with her.

The next day the Porker twins went to Katie's house for a play date. "Look at our new bathing suits!" Belinda said. "Do you have a new one?"

"Our grandma's having a pool party for our birthday," Brendan said.

Katie didn't want to admit that her only bathing suit was a faded purple striped one. And it was too small.

"I don't want to go to Brendan and Belinda's birthday party," she said that night. "It's going to be at their grandmother's swimming pool. What a dumb place to have it!"

Mrs. Catz sighed. "Katie, it's time you learned to swim. I've signed you up for swimming lessons with Patsy Polarbear. She taught the twins."

"I can't go to the town pool. My bathing suit is too small," mumbled Katie.

"That's why I bought you a new one," said her mother.

Katie wasn't at all happy when she got
to the town pool—even though Patsy Polarbear,
the swimming teacher, looked cool and was
very friendly.

Katie was even more unhappy when
her mother blew a kiss and left.

Patsy Polarbear admired the seashells on Katie's new bathing suit. "Come sit with me, Katie," she said. "We can get to know each other. What's your favorite cartoon on TV? Mine's *Submarine Sal*."

Katie didn't want to be rude, so she sat next to Patsy, but she wouldn't put her feet in the water.

"Put your feet in the water and cool off," Patsy said.

Katie shook her head. But soon it got so hot that she put one toe in. Patsy was right. Katie felt cooler right away.

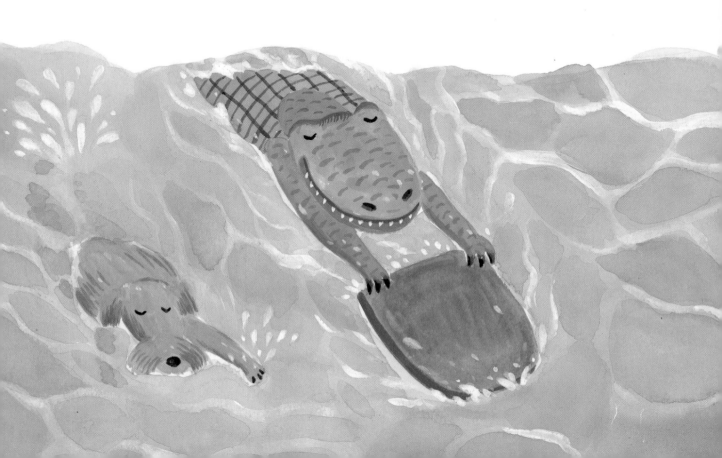

Maybe I'll put one foot in, she thought.

"I'm going to cool off some more," Patsy said, and dropped into the water.

Katie saw that it wasn't deep, but she heard
a gurgling noise she didn't like. It came from a
drain on the side of the pool. "Can sea monsters
come in from there?" she asked Patsy.

"No. But why don't you check it out for
yourself?" said Patsy.

Katie reached into the water. She didn't feel any sea monsters coming through the drain, not even tiny ones. But she yanked her hand out as fast as she could, just to be on the safe side.

"Hey! You splashed me!" Patsy cried. "You won't do that again. I'll hide!"

Patsy dunked her head.

She looked so funny underwater that Katie
started to laugh.

As soon as Patsy bobbed up, Katie kicked
and splashed her again and again.

SPLASH!
SPLASH!
SPLASH!

She even splashed herself. Soon her new
bathing suit was all wet.

"I'll bet you can't splash your own face," said Patsy.

"Oh yes I can," said Katie, and she went splish-splash, splish-splash until her face was all wet.

"You've got a good kick," said Patsy. "But I'll bet you can't do this." She stroked with her arms.

"Oh yes I can!"
said Katie as she
stroked in the air.

Patsy admitted she stroked
very well. "Do you think you
can do it in the water?"

"No, I'll sink," said Katie.

"I won't let you," said Patsy.

"Promise?" asked Katie.

"I promise," said Patsy, and she lifted Katie into the water.

Katie found that she could stroke and kick in the water just as well as she could out of it.

"Let's play Swish! Swish!" Patsy took Katie's hands in hers and twirled her round and round in the water. Katie laughed and laughed. So did Patsy.

Then they played Dunk! Dunk!, and Katie held her breath. She dunked her head just like Patsy did. She wasn't scared. She was having fun.

Suddenly her mother was there, and it was time to go home.

"Good work, Katie! See you Friday," said Patsy.

When Katie came for her next lesson, Patsy
was lying on her back in the water. She looked
very peaceful. "Hi, Katie. Yum—I see a delicious-
looking vanilla ice-cream cone up in the clouds!
Why don't you float and tell me what you see?
Come on in. I'll hold you," she said.

Patsy put her hands under Katie's back and held her as she lay on top of the water with her legs out straight. Katie stretched her arms and looked up at the sky. One cloud was shaped like a big fish.

She didn't notice when Patsy slowly moved her hands away. But Katie didn't sink.

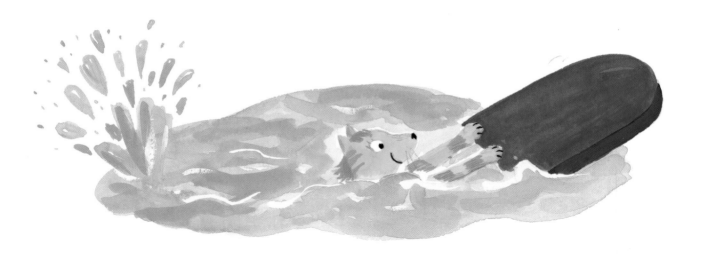

That same day, Katie learned to hold on to a kickboard. She kicked her way across the entire shallow end of the pool.

After that, Katie couldn't wait for her swimming lessons. She practiced kicking. She practiced stroking with one arm while she held on to the kickboard with the other.

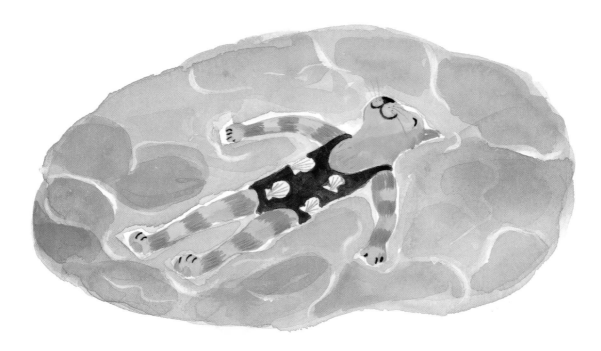

She practiced floating on her back and looking at the clouds. She practiced holding her breath and blowing her breath out when her face was in the water.

One day Katie kicked, and stroked, and breathed all by herself.

"Hooray, Katie! Good swimming!" Patsy cried. Everyone at the pool clapped. Even Chip.

Katie couldn't believe it. But it was true. She was swimming!

On Saturday morning Katie's parents came to the pool with her. "Mom! Dad! Look at me!" said Katie. She swam all the way across the shallow end of the pool.

Katie's parents were mighty proud of her. So was Patsy.

And Katie couldn't wait to go to Brendan
and Belinda's birthday party.